THE TIME WARP TRIO series

Knights of the Kitchen Table

The Not-So-Jolly Roger

The Good, the Bad, and the Goofy

Your Mother Was a Neanderthal

2095

Tut, Tut

Summer Reading Is Killing Me!

It's All Greek to Me

See You Later, Gladiator

Sam Samurai

Hey Kid, Want to Buy a Bridge?

THE TIME WARP TRIO

Viking It
& Liking It

by Jon Scieszka

illustrated by Adam McCauley

SCHOLASTIC INC.
New York Toronto London Auckland Sydney
Mexico City New Delhi Hong Kong Buenos Aires

ISBN 0-439-67974-5

12 11 10 9 8 7 6   8 9/0

Printed in the U.S.A.   40

First Scholastic printing, September 2004

Set in Sabon

To my always exploring, adventuring
Viking dottir—Casey.

J. S.

For the Jefferson Junior
Cyclones

A. M.

ONE

Thunder boomed, then faded to a rumble. Black clouds whipped across the sky. Gray waves crashed on the sand.

Fred, Sam, and I stood on a cold, dark beach. We looked at the ocean. We looked at each other. We knew we weren't in Fred's room anymore. And that's about all we knew.

Sam pushed up his glasses. He wrapped Fred's zebra-pattern bedspread tighter around himself. He would have looked funny . . . if he hadn't looked so mad.

"Joe?" said Sam.

"Yeah?"

"Why are we standing on a cold beach?"

"I really don't know. I was just—"

"Joe?" said Sam.

"Yeah?"

1

"Was that green time warping mist I saw leaking out of your backpack?"

"Yeah, well I had to put *The Book* somewhere. My little sister keeps snooping—"

"Joe?" said Sam.

"Yeah?"

"Hey, at least for once I didn't do anything," said Fred.

"I didn't do anything either," I said. "I was just watching. What did I do?"

Sam held up one hand for quiet. He looked calm. He looked way too calm.

The storm moved out over the ocean. Sun broke through the clouds. One last roll of thunder rumbled in the distance.

"Once again," said Sam, looking like some crazy zebra-robed king, "you guys have warped me into some weird time and place that is probably dangerous to my health."

"We didn't do anything," said Fred, punching Sam in the shoulder. "You were the one saying 'Thursday Thursday Thursday' over and over again like some weirdo. You probably did it."

Sam tried to punch Fred back, but missed when he got stuck in his zebra cape. "I did not. And even if I did, a person should be able to say a regular word without getting sucked back in time to who-knows-when to be attacked by who-knows-what."

Sam's voice was getting louder and screechier. And if you know Sam, you know this is not a good thing. I tried to calm him down

"This isn't so dangerous. We're on a beach. The sun is out now."

Fred tried to help. "Yeah. We've time-warped into a lot worse spots. Like how about that time we warped right into the Black Knight? Or that gladiator?"

Sam didn't say anything.

Fred and I looked out over the ocean. Sam stood facing us, just staring. Not a good sign.

"We'll find *The Book* and get right back to Fred's house in a second," I said. "This probably isn't even a real time warp. I'll bet it's just a mistake. We've probably gone to next Thursday, or last Thursday, or some other Thursday."

Sam sat down in the sand. He put his head in his hands. "Why me?" he said.

That's when Fred and I looked over the top of Sam's head and saw the long wooden boat headed right for our beach. The oars, the striped sail, and the dragon-head front looked terribly familiar. I had seen this in pictures and comics. But something was missing. Maybe it wasn't what I thought it was.

"Uh . . . Sam?"

"Leave me alone."

"Vikings had warships with oars and sails, right?"

"Yeah."

"And Vikings had shields and axes and swords, right?"

4

"Yeah."

"And Vikings had helmets with horns, right?"

"No," said Sam. "That is a common misconception. And it's also not true that Vikings were just bloodthirsty raiders. They were excellent shipbuilders, clever traders, and brave explorers." Sam looked up at me and Fred. "Hey wait a minute. Why are you so interested in Vikings?"

Fred pointed behind Sam to the warship full of guys with shields and axes and swords headed toward us. "I don't see any helmets with horns."

"Maybe they are just well-armed explorers and traders," I said.

Sam turned around.

"*Ahhhhhhh!* Vikings!" he screamed.

Sam jumped up. Sam spun around in circles. Sam screamed some more.

And then he really lost it.

"Vikings!" yelled Sam.

And I guessed they were. And I guessed they didn't wear horns on their helmets. And I guessed we were about to find out if they were brave explorers or bloodthirsty raiders.

TWO

But before we get Vikinged all over the beach, I'd like to explain exactly what happened. Then you tell me how three regular guys from Brooklyn ended up face to face with a boatload of Vikings from a thousand years ago.

It all started at Fred's house. Sam and I were hanging out with Fred. We were playing his older brother's game, NFL Smash. It's a pretty good game. You can make your own football team, smash tackle guys, do victory dances in the end zone.

We only got to play because Fred's brother wasn't home. Fred said if his brother caught us, he would NFL smash us. Sam and Fred played the first game, while I kept a lookout for Fred's brother.

Sam ran his quarterback around the left side. He faked a handoff, then heaved a bomb. It looked like his receiver was there for an easy grab. But

Fred's defender tackled the guy with a giant boom just as the ball landed. Fumble. The crowd went wild. Fred's man scooped up the loose ball and ran it all the way into the end zone.

"Touchdown!" yelled Fred. He jumped up and did the same goofy dance as his guy on screen. "Your team is so ugly, they have to sneak up on their mirror."

"Oh yeah?" said Sam. "Your team is so dumb, they went to the library for a book of matches."

"Your teams are both so lame," I added, "they dialed information to get the number for 911."

And that's pretty much how the afternoon went.

So how did we get from trash talking and NFL game playing to time traveling and real live Vikings?

Good question. It's also a little embarrassing.

The short answer is: a book.

The long answer is: *The Book*. A dark blue book with strange silver writing and symbols on it that my uncle Joe gave me for my birthday. You should probably also know that my uncle Joe is a magician, and that this particular *Book* is a magic book. Don't ask me how, but this *Book* can warp time and space.

The embarrassing part is that *The Book* has warped Fred and Sam and me all over time and space, and we still don't know how it works. Sometimes we see a picture. Sometimes all it takes is a word. The next thing you know—green time traveling mist leaks out of *The Book*, and we're thousands of years back in the Stone Age, or a hundred years forward in the future.

8

The one thing we do know is that the only way to get back home to our time is to use *The Book* in the other time.

Simple, right?

The other small problem is that *The Book* always vanishes when we warp. We have to find it. And it seems like that's when we run into trouble— trouble like black knights or gladiators or Vikings.

You can see why Sam isn't too crazy about time warping.

I promised him I would figure out more of the rules of *The Book*, but I had to finish my math homework, and then we had that story for English, and then I put *The Book* in my backpack to hide it from my little sister who's always snooping around my room. . . .

So it wasn't my fault, right?

I remember Sam and Fred played the rest of their game. I was just flicking through the teams to pick mine. I stopped at the Minnesota Vikings. But I didn't click on them. And nothing funny happened.

Sam wrapped himself in Fred's zebra-striped bedspread. He was looking through his homework planner and asked, "What day is this?"

"Thursday," I said.

"Thursday, Thursday, Thursday," said Sam, flipping through his notebooks. "Hey. Did you ever say a word over and over so many times it didn't make any sense?"

"That makes about as much sense as you usually do," said Fred, lining up his offense.

"No really," said Sam. "Listen—Thursday Thursday—"

Sam was right. The sound didn't make any sense.

But the next sound made even less sense. Without warning, a huge thunder *ba-roooom* filled the air.

A bit of green mist leaked out of my backpack on the floor.

Fred, Sam, and I all saw it.

Another *booom* of thunder filled the air. A cloud of green time-traveling mist filled the room. And the next thing we knew, we were standing on a cold, dark beach, looking at the ocean.

So I didn't pick Vikings, right?

Fred didn't wish for Vikings, right?

But Sam chanted "Thursday." Thunder rumbled. *The Book* time-warped us.

And guess what we got?

THREE

Vikings, a whole boatload of them, hit the beach and charged straight for us.

No horned helmets. But every one of them waved a sword, a spear, an ax, or at least a knife. They looked pretty bloodthirsty to me.

The rest of my first look at real Vikings was a swirl of long hair and beards, capes, belts, and furs. Whatever it was they were yelling sounded more like raiding than trading.

"It's a Viking blitz," said Fred. "We can't take this rush. End run for those trees over there . . . now!"

It was a good play. It could have gone all the way. Fred and I grabbed Sam by both ends of his zebra bedspread. We ran left. But Sam ran right. We fell in a pile. The Vikings had us downed.

"Fourth and long," said Fred, looking at the sharp edge of an ax.

"Maybe we can punt," I said.

Sam spazzed out under Fred's bedspread, making crazy sounds. He jumped up and staggered around in a blind circle. His head popped out. He took one look at the spears and swords and axes. Then Sam stopped, and I don't know why, but he took a deep breath—then let out one long crazy wild animal "raaarrrrrhhhhh!"

The Vikings stared at this nutty kid in a zebra-striped bedspread. One of them yelled back.

Sam flapped his bedspread and roared again, "Raaarrrhh!"

A few of the Viking guys banged their swords and shields together and gave a "rraahh!" back.

"Rooooaaaahhh!" tried Sam.

"Roooaaahh!" yelled a couple of Vikings. The whole crew laughed. They dropped down their weapons, elbowed each other, and pointed at Sam.

"What the heck is going on?" whispered Fred.

"I have no idea," I whispered back. "But it looks good for our team."

A tall man with light reddish hair slid his sword into his belt. He held out his hand to Sam.

"Brave warrior, take my hand," he said in a deep voice. "By Thor's hammer, you must be one mad

14

berserker to challenge my whole crew unarmed." The Viking showed us the silver hammer-shaped piece hanging from a cord around his neck.

"Ch-challenge?" said Sam. He shook the Viking's hand in a daze.

The Viking looked more closely at Sam's bed-spread. "Only a berserker could make himself that crazy before a battle. But what strange bearskin is this? What land is this?"

"We were going to ask you the same thing," said Sam. He pushed his glasses up on his nose.

The Viking leader looked around our clump of land sticking out into the water.

"We have come from our home in Greenland, searching for new lands. We have found Rockland. We have found Woodland." The Viking spotted a clump of bushes with small grape-sized berries. "We will call this land Vinland."

"Vinland?" said Sam. "Really? That's us. I mean that's where we live. Vinland is what the Vikings called North America. So you guys really are Vikings. And you really did come to North America."

A small blond-haired Viking in a purple cloak stepped up. He held out his hands, then spoke in a weird sing-songy voice.

"Bold Leif   found the New World.
He called it   Vinland.
Then he smashed   ten thousand warriors,
Using only   one hand."

"What?" said Fred.

"Oh don't mind him," said the Viking leader. "That's Bullshik, my official skald—that's a poet. My dad got him for me. Thought I should have someone working on the saga of my life."

"It seems like he exaggerates a little bit," said Sam.

"Yeah, that's the poetry part, I guess," said the Viking, looking a little embarrassed. Bullshik looked annoyed.

I didn't want the Viking leader to feel bad enough to start making the smashing part of the saga come true, so I stepped forward. A cool blast of ocean wind blew sand over our sneakers. I still couldn't figure out how we had gotten warped here into Viking times, but I did figure out that the sooner we found *The Book* and got back home, the better.

"Well, it's been very nice meeting you, Mr. Bold Leif," I said. "But we really have to go. Got a big game to finish. So do you or any of your guys have a small blue *Book*?"

The Viking leader looked confused.

"You know," said Fred. "Pages with writing on it."

"Scrolls?" said Sam. "Maybe a sealskin with pictures on it or something like that? Someplace you write down your stories?"

The Vikings looked at each other. Now they all looked confused.

17

"I am the keeper and speaker of stories," said Bullshik in that goofy voice of his. "No one writes stories on skins. Vikings live brave lives. Their stories live on in the sagas the skalds tell."

"Oh no," said Sam. "We're back before writing. How are we going to find *The Book* if they don't have books? We're doomed, as usual."

Bullshik the skald decided to give us another example of his saga telling.

"Leif the Bold,   Leif the Lucky,
Rode the waves.   It was fun.
Clever Bullshik   told the fine saga
Of Leif,   Erik's son."

I was still thinking we were doomed forever . . . and were double doomed to have to hear bad poetry forever . . . when Sam perked up.

"Did you say Leif, Erik's son?" said Sam. "Leif Eriksson?"

"Leif the Bold, Leif the Lucky—" Bullshik started again.

Sam cut him off. "We're saved! This is Leif Eriksson, you guys. You know—Leif Eriksson who finds North America. We are from America. *The*

Book must be in America. We take Leif there and get *The Book*."

Now the Viking leader looked completely confused. "What is this America?"

Sam grabbed a stick and sketched a map in the sand.

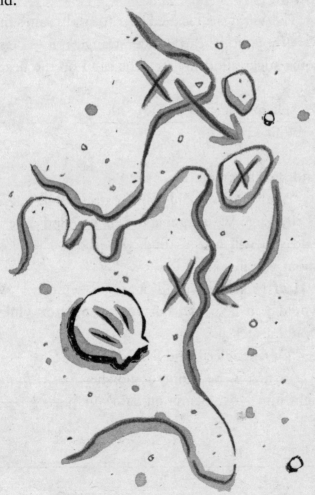

"You call it Vinland. We call it North America. The way I figure it—we're somewhere around the year one thousand. And we are somewhere in Canada. Maybe Newfoundland, here. Maybe Nova Scotia, here. All we have to do is head south toward New York."

The Vikings all leaned over to study Sam's map.

I thought I heard some strange noises. I saw some sticks suddenly stab the sand on the beach.

"Flight swift,   lion's tooth,
Whizzers—"

said Bullshik, pointing.

"Yeah yeah," said Sam, cutting Bullshik off. "Leif, listen. We are going to help you find America. And you will help us find *The Book*. They'll talk about you in sagas forever. Okay?"

Leif Eriksson looked at us suspiciously. "Why would you help me, but your people of Vinland would attack us?"

"Our people?" said Sam.

An arrow flew out of nowhere and *thunked* right into Nova Scotia on Sam's map.

"Wind riders,   air strikers . . ."

sang Bullshik.

Leif pointed to a swarm of Indian war canoes pulling around the far shore. Arrows flew in a cloud from "our people" in the canoes.

"Head stabbers,   bloody hole makers—"

said Bullshik.

"Those are called arrows, you dimbulb," said Fred. "Why didn't you say so?"

"And those are the people who already live here," said Sam.

"It looks like we're not going to discover Vinland," I said. "It's discovered us."

FOUR

"Ten thousand   mad skraelings
Swarmed Leif   giving shout.
He swung   his Skull-Crusher,
And knocked them   all out,"

Bullshik chanted.

Leif and his Vikings raised their shields overhead. More arrows (or wind riders, or stab-you-in-the-headers, or whatever you want to call them) struck the sand and thunked into the shields.

"Dude, that is terrible poetry," said Fred. "And it's not even close to true."

"Back to the longship, men," yelled Leif.

The Vikings took off running.

"Hey, what about us?" yelled Sam.

"You Vinlanders are crazy . . . and dangerous," shouted Leif. "You can keep your New Land. We're going back home to Greenland."

Sam, Fred, and I looked back at the war-whooping "Vinlanders" hopping out of the canoes. We looked forward at the Viking Greenlanders climbing into their longboat.

"Well, *The Book* could be in Greenland," said Sam. "Let's get out of here."

We ran our fastest play ever—the Dash-to-the-Viking-Ship, Jump-In, Push-Off, and Watch-Vikings-Row-Like-Crazy play.

And that's how Fred, Sam, and I found ourselves sitting on the deck of a real Viking longboat headed toward chilly Greenland, leaving Vinland

and a very angry bunch of original Vinlanders far, far behind.

Fred's football jersey flapped in the wind. I buttoned up my shirt. Sam pulled his zebra cloak a little tighter.

"I wish I'd dressed a little warmer for a Viking adventure," I said.

"I wish someone had warned me we were going on a Viking adventure," said Sam.

"Aw, come on," said Fred. "This should be fun."

Sam shook his head. "If you had a brain, you'd be dangerous."

"Take off your mask, Halloween is over," answered Fred.

"I don't know what we'd do without you," said Sam. "But we could give it a try."

I suddenly noticed no one was rowing anymore. Everyone was looking at us. And looking at us in a weird way.

"Hey guys," I said to Sam and Fred.

"You're so lame," said Fred, "You'd need a bazooka to—"

"Guys!" I yelled.

Fred and Sam stopped trashing each other, and realized every Viking was looking at us.

"With the New Land   discovered,
Leif sailed   home free.
But first he   and his ferocious warriors
Tossed three sacrifices   to the sea,"

sing-sang Bullshik.

"Three sacrifices to the sea," I said. "Ha, that is a very good poem. Very exciting."

Three huge Vikings grabbed us from behind and lifted us off our feet. Another Viking with a nasty white scar all down his face, right through his eye, pulled out his short sword.

I suddenly realized we were about to become the first verse of Bullshik's saga that was actually true.

"Hey, wait a minute," said Sam. "You can't sacrifice us to the sea. I might go berserk, remember?"

Leif the Bold stood in front of us. "No extra room or extra supplies on a longboat. You must be good with an oar or good with an ax to be worth keeping for the long voyage home."

"Oh, we are completely worth keeping," said Fred. "Isn't that right, Joe?"

"Yeah, Joe," said Sam. "Show them a little time warp magic . . . quick."

"Magic?" said Leif Eriksson, suddenly looking interested.

"You young Vinlanders know the runes ever-lasting, the runes life-giving?" said Bullshik, not looking like he quite believed it.

The three large Vikings lowered us to the deck with new respect.

"Heck yeah, we know the ruined whatever-you-said," said Fred. "Joe knows all that stuff. He got *The Book* from his uncle Joe, you know."

"How to tell   men's thoughts?
Blunt sword blades,   calm the wild waves?
Understand   the cries of birds?"

asked Bullshik, quoting Viking poems again.

"Sure," said Sam. "That's nothing for Time Warp guys like us, right, Joe?"

Everyone looked at me.

The Viking longboat bobbed up and down in the gentle waves.

The Vikings' thoughts were easy to tell—Leif was surprised. Bullshik was suspicious. And every-one else was looking forward to either a good trick . . . or a chance to "toss three sacrifices into the sea."

I stared at Thor's hammer hanging from a cord around Leif's neck. I tried to think.

A seagull cried somewhere above the ship.

And I could have sworn it said, "So long, suckers. . . ."

FIVE

The seagull's cry died in the breeze.

"Amaze our peepers,   fill our ear sails.
Or taste the hammer   on your land of brains,"

said Bullshik.

"What?" said Fred.

"He wants to see a good trick or they smash in our heads," said Sam, getting the hang of Viking poetry.

"That's what I thought he said," said Fred.

Fred and Sam looked at me.

I looked around at my audience. This was one rough bunch. And anybody who would sail across the ocean in a boat this small and this open had to be a little crazy, too.

I started talking to stall for time. I had to come

up with a trick good enough to impress a bunch of Vikings who looked like they might really enjoy using their axes, spears, and swords.

"Vikings and gentleman, so nice you could be here today. I would like to show you just one of our many incredible powers. So you definitely don't want to sacrifice us or smash in our land of brains."

The Incredible Pick-Any-Card trick seemed less than incredible for this crowd. The Amazing Bouncing Handkerchief suddenly didn't seem so amazing.

One of the biggest Viking audience members picked up Sam with one hand.

"Can you fly?"

The other Vikings laughed.

"Hey, hey, be careful," said Sam. "I get mad berserk seasick."

I watched the Viking lifting Sam up and down . . . and then I knew the perfect trick.

"No, we don't usually fly," I said. "But we can call on the power to become heavy as stone, more heavy than a giant, too heavy for any man to lift."

"Only dwarves   come from stone.
First man   and first woman
Are from   the armpit sweat of a giant,"

Bullshik recited.

"Well yes, of course," I said. "Everyone knows that people come from the armpit sweat of a giant."

"We do?" asked Fred.

"Urg," said Sam in midair.

"And usually it's only dwarves who know the heavy power of stone. But observe!" I held my arms bent at the elbow, right next to my body. "Have your strongest man lift me by my elbows."

Everyone turned to look at the giant guy holding the steering oar.

"Skrolf! Skrolf the Beast!"

Skrolf the Beast clomped over. I think his one arm was bigger around than my whole body. He put his meaty hands under my elbows. He lifted me like I was a toothpick.

I suddenly had second thoughts about my Heavier-than-Stone trick. I realized I had never tried it out using a real giant.

"Now," I said,

"Hocus pocus   third and long.
Power of stone   hut hut hike."

I put my hands on the top of my shoulders. But

this time I held my elbows out forward, in front of my body.

"Let two of your strongest men lift me by my elbows now."

Another beefy Viking, who was huge enough to play in the NFL, flipped back his cape. He and Skrolf the Beast each grabbed an elbow. I planted my feet, and held my breath. They tried to lift me.

They tried, and tried, and tried some more. The Vikings roared in amazement. They banged their

shields. They hooted at Skrolf and his pal. But they couldn't lift me.

Even Bullshik was impressed.

"A small sapling   was Joe.
His chants   did make him
A mighty stone."

I nodded. I wasn't going to tell him it was actually more a center of gravity thing. If your elbows are down next to your waist, they are in line with your center of gravity. It makes you easy to lift. But move your elbows out forward, and the lift is impossible for any human.

"Fantastic," said Leif.

"Joe! Joe! Joe of Stone! Joe of Stone!" chanted the Vikings.

"With Joe of Stone   and Berserker Sam
Strong-Hearted Leif   kicked the butt
Of the foul   Snake-in-the-Grass."

"Thanks. Thanks," I said, giving a little bow. "Happy to help. But what was that about a foul snake in the grass?"

"Grim Snake-in-the-Grass," said Leif Eriksson. "My cousin, set on revenge for a sheep he said my brother once took from him."

"Well, he doesn't sound like such a nice guy," I said.

Sam threw a left, then threw a right. "I'm sure he'd be no trouble for us. Like Bullshik says, we'd help Leif kick his butt if we ever ran into him."

That's when I noticed the rest of the Vikings taking their shields out of the rack on the sides of the ship. They put on helmets, tested axes. The oarsmen turned our boat to face the edge of the bay.

Bullshik pointed. We saw another Viking longboat, black and sinister looking, heading right for us. Then he said the words we didn't want to hear: "Grim Snake-in-the-Grass. This will be good. You can use your powers of the runes everlasting."

"Uh . . . I didn't know Vikings fought other Vikings," I said.

Fred picked up a wooden club and found an extra helmet.

SIX

Leif's men were ready for battle in about five seconds.

"Let Odin, the god of war, be with us," said Leif. "Remember—if you die bravely in battle, the Valkyries will come and take you to Odin's great hall, Valhalla."

"What the heck is a Valkyrie?" said Fred.

"Women warriors who fly over battles on their horses," said Bullshik. "They collect only the warriors who die bravely."

"Die bravely," said Leif. "And we'll drink from the skulls of our enemies in Valhalla for all time."

The Vikings cheered and clashed their weapons against shields.

"Now that sounds like a lot of fun," said Sam from under his bedspread. "But let's not go to Valhalla and meet Odin just yet. I don't think I'm quite ready."

"Let's see what they've got," said Fred, fixing his helmet.

"Joe of Stone   spoke the runes.
He batted away   the storm of arrows.
He told the sea to   swallow Grim's ship,"

chanted Bullshik, warming up.

Leif tested the edge of his sword with his thumb and nodded.

"Gee, I'd really like to help," I said. "But I haven't been practicing my batting away arrows or opening up the sea."

Grim's sleek black ship glided quickly across the bay. The dragon-head front sliced through the waves.

"Look first for the hail of arrows," Leif said to me. "Then the rain of spears. After that they will fight with ax and sword to board us."

"Uh . . . okay," I said.

What else could I say? I had a terrible sinking feeling that Leif and his men were counting on me to actually do something about the "hail of arrows" and "rain of spears." I didn't want to even think about the "ax and sword" fight.

Grim's ship drew close. I could just make out the shape of a short guy in front. Leif stood tall. I ducked behind him and waited for the first arrows of an all-out Viking sea battle.

"Leif!" came a call from the other ship. "Cousin Leif!" shouted the short guy up front.

"He holds a white shield of peace," said Bullshik. "Not the red shield of war."

"Probably a trick," said Leif. "Stand ready."

"It's me—Grim," shouted the little guy. "We will honor you with a feast. Come ashore."

"I don't trust that Grim Snake-in-the-Grass," said Skrolf, our steering oarsman.

Leif waved his sword overhead and showed Grim a fake smile. "I don't either. But it would be an insult and a senseless fight for sure if we refuse."

"So you don't want me to turn their swords to rubber and make the ocean swallow them up?" I said.

Leif didn't, and gave the orders to head for shore.

And that's how, in what seemed like a time warp of its own, we found ourselves in one of the shortest Time Warp chapters ever, and in the middle of a Viking feast, instead of in the middle of a bloody Viking battle at sea.

SEVEN

Fred, Sam, and I sat close to one of the two giant bonfires burning on the beach. We were glad to be warm and dry. We were glad to be feasting with Vikings instead of fighting with them.

"Too bad though," said Sam. He sliced the air with his stick like it was a sword. "I was ready to rumble."

"Ready to rumble up your lunch on my bedspread," said Fred, taking a bite of roast walrus off his stick.

"I'm a berserker," said Sam. "That's how I get ready for battle."

I tried a hunk of the dried reindeer meat supplied by Grim. "Like beef jerky," I said. "Maybe Leif's cousin isn't such a nasty guy after all. He's giving us food and drink. Maybe he has the Viking version of *The Book* to give us."

"Pass me a hunk of that whale blubber," said

Fred. "I say we eat now. Worry about that later."

"Typical," said Sam.

"Mrrrmmmph frwwwbb," answered Fred with a mouthful.

The Vikings seemed to agree with Fred's philosophy of life—eat now and worry later. Vikings from both ships sat around the fires eating and drinking like there was no tomorrow.

Most of Leif's men sat around our fire. Most of Grim's men sat around the other fire. Anyone watching might have thought it was just a friendly Viking family get-together. But I noticed all of Leif's men sitting just like Leif told them to, with their swords and spears within easy reach.

The sun began to sink lower in the sky.

Grim stepped into the light between the two fires. He was a very short guy with beady black eyes that seemed to be always moving back and forth. He did look kind of snake-ish. He raised his drinking horn. "To my cousin Leif, and the end of our feud."

"To Leif," shouted the Vikings. And they drained their drinking horns.

Leif stood up. "To Cousin Grim."

"To Grim!" Everyone drank.

A couple of Grim's men moved around the fires. They filled everyone's drinking horns out of small wooden barrels.

One of the guys, with his beard neatly braided into a point, pushed a horn into each of our hands.

"Oh, no thanks," I said. "We're too—"

"Very bad manners," growled the bearded Viking in a very deep voice. He put one hand on his sword handle.

We each took a horn. He filled them up with yellow-brown liquid.

"To Odin, god of war!" someone shouted.

"To Odin, god of war!" everyone shouted back.

Fred, Sam, and I sipped our drinks.

"Bleahhh!" said Fred. He spit his drink into the sand behind us when the drink guy wasn't looking. "What is this—seal juice?"

"It's probably mead," said Sam, always our expert. "It's like a kind of beer."

"To Thunder God Thor!" someone else shouted.

"To Thunder God Thor!" came the answer. We pretended to drink.

The Vikings toasted and drank and toasted and drank some more. The sun went down. The Viking beach party got darker and louder. The toasts seemed to be getting more personal, and a little bit nasty.

"To Leif's little warriors."

"To Grim's buttkissers."

Bullshik stood up and raised his drinking horn. That's when I knew things were about to get really out of control.

"Grim's men are strong   to the death.
At least that's true   about their breath."

Leif's men laughed. Grim's men did not.

A scrawny-looking guy jumped up next to Bullshik, flipped back his sealskin cloak, and struck a pose.

"Who the heck is this guy?" said Fred.

"That's Grim's skald—Fulluvit," said Skrolf.

"You're kidding," said Sam. "I didn't think anyone could have a name worse than Bullshik."

Skrolf gave Sam a blank look. He didn't get it.

"Never mind," said Sam. "Go, Bullshik! Give him heck!"

Fulluvit held his pose.

"To Leif and his men   advice before speaking:
Wipe your nose   your brains are leaking."

Grim's men howled and toasted. Leif's men didn't.

Then things got nasty. Bullshik rhymed something about Grim's men with Snake-in-the-Grass. Fulluvit toasted back his own rhyme about nose pickers.

A few of Leif's men at our fire picked up swords and spears. One of Grim's men slowly put his ax over one shoulder.

"Uh-oh," said Sam, sinking under his bedspread. "Things are getting ugly."

"Vikings! Brothers!" shouted someone. It was Grim. He stood between Bullshik and Fulluvit. "This is no way to toast fellow Vikings. Urlf— bring my special brew."

Urlf, who looked as ugly as his name sounded, came out with another keg under his arm. He filled the drinking horns of Leif and all of Leif's men.

"I was saving this special brew," said Grim. "But nothing is too good for our friends and fellows."

This idea seemed to satisfy everyone.

Urlf got another keg and filled the drinking horns of Grim and Grim's men.

"Skoal!" toasted Grim.

"Skoal!" toasted everyone in return.

And about ten seconds later, Leif and his men started dropping like flies in cold weather. They fell to the sand.

"We've been poisoned," said Bullshik, throwing his horn.

"Coward," said Leif. He pulled his sword, but fell over before he could use it.

Skrolf and a few more of Leif's men stayed standing long enough to draw their weapons and slash a few times with an ax or spear. Then they dropped to the sand, too.

Sam, Fred, and I had poured out the nasty brew while everyone else was drinking. Now we were the only ones standing, facing Grim Snake-in-the-Grass and twenty armed Vikings with one zebra bedspread, Fred's wooden club, and any trick I could think of in the next twenty seconds.

We didn't need a skald to tell us:

Things look bad   for Bold Joe, Sam, and Fred.
Vikings call it Valhalla.   We call it dead.

EIGHT

The sun came up blood red the next morning. And we didn't feel so hot either.

Fred, Sam, and I stood on the beach with our hands tied in front of us. Leif, Bullshik, and the rest of Leif's crew sat with their hands tied behind them.

Grim and his Vikings had not been impressed by Sam's zebra bedspread, Fred's wooden club, or my offer to do a little magic. In fact, we never had a chance. They tied our hands. They forced us to drink. And that's the last thing we remembered.

Now Grim and his skald, Fulluvit, walked up and down in front of us.

"Leif and his losers, you are about to be executed. No one will remember you. Fulluvit will tell the saga of Grim Snake-in-the-Grass—the Viking who discovered the New World."

Grim posed for a second.

"Any questions? No, I didn't think so. My swordsman Gunnar will now chop off your heads."

"You are a coward, and a dishonor to all Vikings," said Leif. "Give us our weapons. Let us die fighting and enter Valhalla."

"Or we could try to think of something else," said Sam. He looked completely crazy with his hair flying every which way. "No need to start chopping heads or calling in the Valkyries."

Bullshik looked at us. "That's right," he said.

"Grim, you don't know the power of the runes that these Vinlanders know."

Grim walked over to stand in front of Fred, Sam, and me. Small waves splashed on the shore. Seagulls called. I still had no idea what they were saying. But I had a bad feeling that I could tell the future, and it had me trying to think of a good trick.

Grim's dark beady eyes looked into mine. He wasn't much taller than me. "So what would you know? Would you tell me a poem—like Egil told Erik Bloodaxe—so I would spare your heads?"

"No, I am the skald," said Bullshik. "I would tell a tale—"

"I know, I know," said Grim. "I've heard enough of your poems. Start one more, and Gunnar will chop off your head first."

Bullshik looked offended. But he knew better than to annoy Grim any more. "Fine. But Joe the Stone will challenge you. He will show the impossible if you will then set us free."

"He will?" asked Grim, smiling an ugly smile.

"I will?" I said, thinking the impossible was pretty impossible.

"He will," said Fred, jabbing me with his elbow.

51

"And I will recover a fumble and hand off to our quarterback."

I wondered what the heck Fred was talking about. Fred glanced down. I looked down. I saw a knife, half buried in the sand under Fred's foot. I got it. He wanted me to distract Grim and his men so he could hand off the knife to Leif.

"He'd better," said Sam. " 'Cause if I find myself in Valhalla, I am going to be really annoyed, even if I do get to drink out of skulls."

"So?" said Grim.

I casually moved away from Fred so Grim and his men would have to turn to watch me.

The seagulls called, circling above us.

I still had no idea what impossible trick I was going to do. I used what I had already heard from Bullshik that they might believe. "I can calm the waves and turn away arrows," I said. "But first I must listen to what the birds are telling me."

Right on cue, the seagulls called. Behind Grim and his Vikings, I saw Fred crouch down.

"Aha," I said. I looked up to make everyone else look up.

"Ah yes," I said. I tried to think of an "impossible" trick.

The seagulls screeched.

"I see," I said.

The seagulls screeched.

"You don't say," I said.

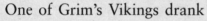

Gunnar started to swing his ax. I knew I couldn't keep this up much longer.

One of Grim's Vikings drank from a horn. Another Viking put his helmet down on the sand. I looked at the drink and the helmet. That gave me the idea for my "impossible" trick. It wasn't perfect, but . . .

"Give me a drink and a helmet," I said. "And I will show you the impossible. Place the drink under the helmet. And even with my hands tied in front of me like this, I will drink from it without touching the helmet."

Grim looked doubtful.

One of his men jammed a drinking horn in the sand, then covered it with a helmet.

I held my tied hands together over the helmet, and stalled for as much time as I could for Fred and Leif to get free.

"Watch me closely, very closely," I said, trying to keep everyone's eyes on me. I leaned over and stared at the helmet.

"Abracadabra   clink think
Nose picker   butt kicker
Zim zam   drink!"

I closed my eyes and pretended I was sucking the drink through an invisible straw.

"Ah, there," I said, and looked up at Grim.

Grim looked back at me with his snake eyes. He lifted up the helmet.

I grabbed the drinking horn and took a sip.

"See? I drank from the horn without touching the helmet."

54

Grim and his men stared. A few guys laughed when they got it. Then they all started to laugh. All except Grim.

"Very clever," said Grim. "We will honor you by chopping off your head first. Gunnar?"

NINE

So it wasn't my greatest trick ever. But I never expected to get my head chopped off for a bad trick.

Leif stepped forward with his hands still behind his back. I guessed Fred hadn't got the knife to him in time.

"Cousin Grim," said Leif. "So you are both a disgrace and a liar who would not honor your own promise?"

"Leif, you are such a loser," said Grim. "Years from now, no one will even remember your name. It is my name that will live on forever in the saga of Grim who found the New Land. Give them a few verses, Fulluvit."

Fulluvit stood next to Grim and lifted his sharp nose into the air.

"Brave Grim on the ocean   was storm tossed.
Leif and his losers   got themselves lost."

"Wow," said Fred. "You *are* Fulluvit."

Grim turned on Fred. "Maybe your head should be first."

"No, first I have a short verse that might interest you," said Bullshik.

"Bold Leif   with Snake-Biter
Showed Grim   the real fighter."

"Now what is that supposed to mean?" said Grim.

"Yaaaaahhh!" screamed Leif for an answer. It was a true battle cry that both surprised and froze everyone. Fred had got the knife to him and freed everyone's hands while they were watching my trick.

Leif grabbed Grim in a chokehold with the knife to his head.

Grim's men were so shocked, they never had a chance to move.

Skrolf flattened Gunnar and snatched up his sword.

Bullshik sacked Fulluvit.

Leif's men blitzed the rest of Grim's Vikings before anyone could make a move for weapons. Sam hopped around, flapping his zebra bedspread. Fred piled on, then helped tie up Grim and his Vikings with the same ropes that had just been holding us.

In minutes we were standing on the same beach, but in a completely different way. We were free. Grim and his men were the prisoners.

Now the sun didn't look so blood red. It looked kind of wonderful gold.

"Leif the Lucky   was saved
By Vinlander   Fred.
And then   Grim Snake
Lost   his head,"

chanted Bullshik.

"Really?" said Sam.

A soft breeze blew in from the ocean. Leif the Bold looked at Grim and his men, deciding their fate.

"Viking law demands the guilty be punished in a way that fits the crime," said Leif.

The sun looked blood red again.

TEN

The wind picked up. Dark clouds drifted in from the ocean.

"The punishment should fit the crime," said Leif. His long hair and beard streamed in the wind. Leif and his men held their swords, spears, and axes again. Grim and his Vikings stood together in a bunch, their hands tied behind them.

"Chop off their heads like they were going to do to us," said Bullshik. "That fits the crime."

"Or maybe just chop off their hands, 'cause that was what they were going to use to do the crime," said Skrolf thoughtfully.

"Or maybe smash in their brains for thinking up the crime," said an ax-carrying Viking. He demonstrated his smashing chop on a nearby piece of wood.

"Or maybe cut out their tongues for saying the crime," said another guy.

Then Leif's Vikings started thinking up really nasty punishments.

"Or maybe they need a very very long time-out until they learn to get along with others," said Sam.

"Chop off their heads," said Fred.

Leif listened to everyone. He looked over the land, and then out over the ocean. "Yes. I have the punishment to fit the crime."

From the way Leif said it, everyone knew he was in charge. No one asked. No one questioned. But I did wonder—what punishment would fit this crime? And how disgusting would it be?

Grim and his men didn't lose their heads. They didn't lost their hands, their tongues, or any other body parts. Leif had his men untie them. He put them back on their ship with everything except their weapons.

"Grim," said Leif Eriksson. "You wanted so much to tell your saga. You wanted people to re-member your name forever. Your punishment will be to have people remember the saga of what a coward you are forever."

Grim, Fulluvit, and the rest of the Vikings on board looked like they had lost everything. And I guess in a way they had. They would not be

61

remembered as heroes of Viking history. Their names would not live on in any saga.

Leif had shown that he was the real hero without even fighting.

Leif's men pushed the black warship out into the wind-whipped waves. Grim and his men had no choice but to go. Oars stroked the waves. Grim's losers raised the sail and disappeared into the approaching storm.

Leif turned to Fred. "Young warrior, take this." Leif handed Fred the knife with the antler horn handle. The knife that Fred had used to free Leif's hands. The knife that saved all of our heads. "It's name is Snake-Biter."

"Brave Fred, Berserk Sam,   and Magic Joe
Saved Leif and his Vikings.   All will know,"

said Bullshik.

Leif's Vikings began to pack up their ship. They

stowed supplies and clothes in chests they used as seats. They pulled out their long oars.

"So will you go with us back to Greenland? Or stay here in Vinland with your people?" said Leif.

Sam looked nervously down the coast. "Those guys with the bows and arrows? Well, we really don't know them that well. Maybe we should go along with you just to keep you safe for a while."

"Maybe *The Book* will turn up somewhere we go raiding along the way," I said.

Fred slid Snake-Biter into his belt. "Well, let's go a-viking."

I looked over Vinland. It was a wild, empty-looking place. No sign of anything that might be part of a certain *Book*. It looked like it was going to be a while before we got back to our land, our time, and our NFL Smash game.

Leif smiled. "You have proved your worth. Sail with us."

The wind blew a stinging blast of sand down the beach. Dark clouds covered the sky.

I took one last look at land. Skrolf was the last Viking ashore. He was just packing dirt and sand around a big tombstone-shaped rock. He waved us up.

"Come see Skrolf's runestone and then we'll go," said Leif.

"Sure," I said. But I wasn't really in the mood for any more rune tricks.

Fred, Sam, and I walked up the beach with Leif and Bullshik. Skrolf showed off his handiwork. The stone was half buried in the ground. It had what looked like a bunch of chicken tracks carved into it.

"We made it for you," said Skrolf proudly. "Read it."

"Read what?" I said. "I thought you said you didn't write anything down."

"The runes," said Bullshik. He pointed to the chicken-track carvings in the stone.

"I've got some sand in my eye," I said. "Skrolf, you should read it. You did such a nice job carving it."

Skrolf beamed at the compliment. He stood back and read the chicken-track runes.

"Joe, Sam, and Fred were here
With Leif Eriksson and his men
This Thor's day."

64

Thunder rumbled in the sky above.

"What did you say?" said Sam.

"Joe, Sam, and Fred—" Skrolf began again.

"No no no," said Sam. "That last part. Is that what those scratches are? Writing? Runes? Thor's day Thor's day Thorsday?"

Thunder kabooomed.

A faint wisp of green mist snaked around the runestone.

Everything suddenly made sense. Thursday was Thor's day. Thor was the Viking god of thunder. The runes were Viking writing.

So the writing on the runestone was the Viking version of *The Book*. Sam chanting "Thursday" triggered the Viking time warp that got us here. Chanting "Thor's day" with the runes would get us back.

"Thor's day Thor's day Thor's day!" sang Sam, berserking around in his bedspread.

Thunder *boomed*.

A storm of green time-traveling mist swirled up over us.

And we Vikinged out of there, leaving Leif Eriksson to explore Vinland, and Bullshik to tell the strange saga.

ELEVEN

We stood staring at the NFL Smash game. The team jersey on the screen was the Minnesota Vikings. They had horns on their helmets.

"I can't believe it," said Sam.

I said, "I wasn't the one who said Thurs—"

"Don't say it!" yelled Sam, tackling me.

Fred checked his belt. "Aw, I didn't get to keep Snake-Biter."

"You remind me of the Liberty Bell," said Sam. "Half cracked."

"You better not go to the zoo, people will try to feed you," said Fred.

We were so glad to be back in our time, back in Fred's house, and so busy cracking on each other that we never even heard Fred's brother come in.

"What are you little scrubs doing playing my NFL Smash game?" said Fred's big brother Mike. He dropped his gym bag and stood over us, looking bigger than Skrolf. "I should smash you."

Thunder rumbled outside.

I tried to think of what Leif would do in a situation like this. I said,

> "Bold Fred,   Magic Joe,
> Berserker Sam,   I say:
> Sometimes it's   good to run
> And live to fight   another day."

"What?" said Fred's brother.

"Hut hut *hike*!" yelled Fred.

We tried to run for it. I ran left. Sam ran right. Fred ran right up the middle . . . and got caught.

Sam and I couldn't leave Bold Fred all on his own. We had a saga to live. So:

> Magic Joe   and Berserker Sam
> Bounced Fred's   brother off the wall, uh . . .
> Even though   it surely meant
> Early entry to   Valhalla.

Days of the Week

It turns out that four different days of the week are named for four of the main Norse gods.

Thursday comes from "Thor's day."

Tuesday come from "Tyr's day."

Wednesday comes from "Wotan's day" (Wotan is another name for Odin).

And Friday comes from "Freya's day."

So don't be surprised if you find yourself acting like a Viking on Tuesday, Wednesday, Thursday, and Friday.

Figure Out Your Own Viking Name

Leif Eriksson's name is made from his dad's name—Erik. He is Leif, Erik's son. Leif Eriksson.

So if your first name is Fred, and your dad's name is John, your name is Fred Johnsson.

If your first name is Jill, and your dad's name is John, your name is Jill Johnsdottir (John's daughter).

Or you could always go with a nickname. But be careful. There were Vikings who ended up with names like Olaf the Fat, Sven Fork Beard, Flatnose, Bluetooth, and Hairy Pants. I'd hate to see you end up being called something like Fred Hairy Pants for the rest of your life.

Write in Runes

We learn our ABCs.

Vikings who learned to write runes learned their FUTHs.

The basic rune alphabet is called FUTHARK, after its first six letters. The straight lines of the letters make it easy to carve them into wood, horn, or stone.

Be a real Viking and make your own runestone. Translate your name into runes. Carve them into a giant stone. Set your runestone up where people will admire it for thousands of years. Here is an example of an early rune alphabet:

ᚠf ᚢu ᚦth ᚨa ᚱr ᚲk ᚷg

ᚹv,w ᚺh ᚾn ᛁi ᛃj ᛇei ᛈp

ᛉz ᛋs ᛏt ᛒb ᛖe ᛗm ᛚl

ᛜng ᛞd ᛟo

Be a Skald,
Write Your Own Saga

Make up your own saga by thinking of heroic verses for everything you do.

Tell your saga at parties and dinnertime.

Become famous forever . . . or maybe just very annoying for now.

ᛏᛁᛗᛖ ᛞᛟᚱᛋ ᚹᚠᚱᚳ
Time does warp

ᛏᛁᛗᛖ ᛞᛟᚱᛋ ᛒᛖᚾᛞ
Time does bend

ᛟᚢᚱ ᛋᚠᚷᚠ ᛁᛋ ᛞᛟᚾᛖ
Our saga is done

ᚦᛁᛋ ᛁᛋ ᚦᛖ ᛖᚾᛞ
This is the end

73